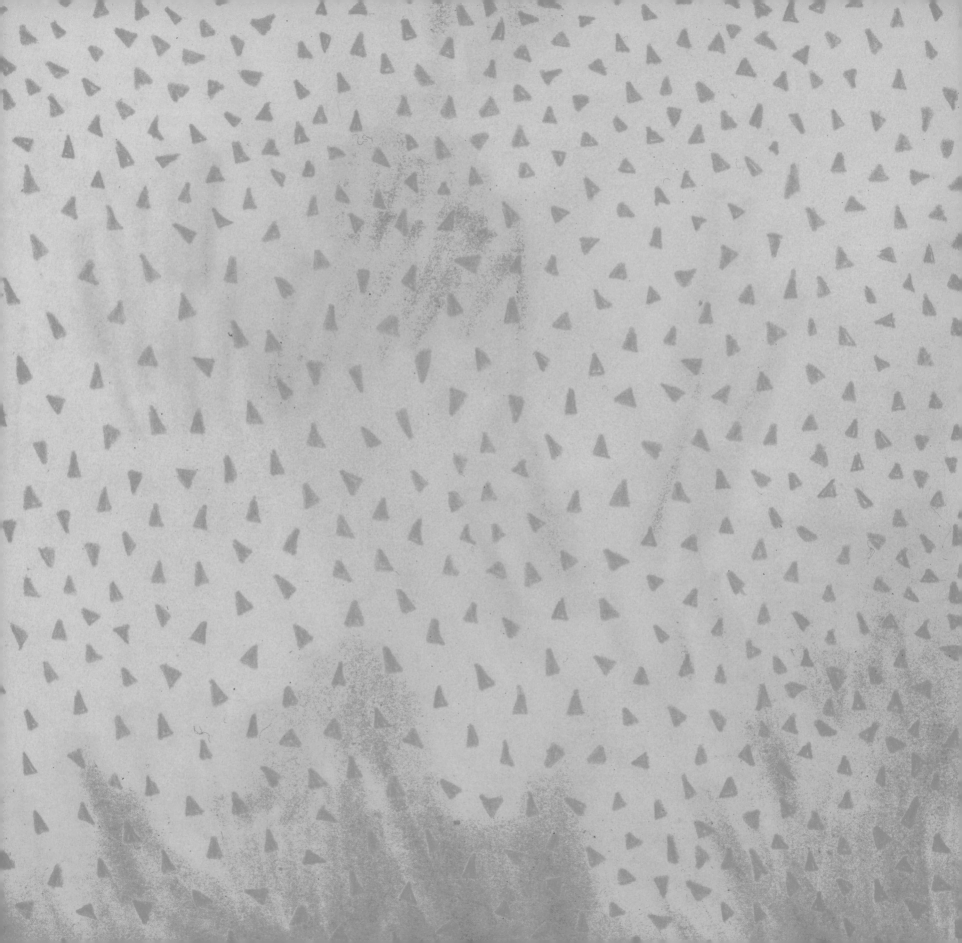

This book belongs to:

_____

To Shirin Shamsi, who taught me to follow my dreams and always believed in me, and to all the children I've ever had the pleasure of teaching, who provided me with stories, surprises, laughter, and daily life lessons – M.H.

For Seamus – may you always find your sun – A.W.

First American edition published in 2024 by
Crocodile Books
An imprint of Interlink Publishing Group, Inc.
46 Crosby Street
Northampton, Massachusetts 01060

www.interlinkbooks.com

Text © Maryam Hassan, 2024
Illustrations © Anna Wilson, 2024

Published simultaneously in Great Britain by Hodder & Stoughton,
an imprint of Hachette Children's Group

Library of Congress Cataloging-in-Publication Data available

ISBN 978-1-62371-693-6

Printed and bound in China

10 9 8 7 6 5 4 3 2 1

MIX
Paper from
responsible sources
FSC
www.fsc.org   FSC® C104740

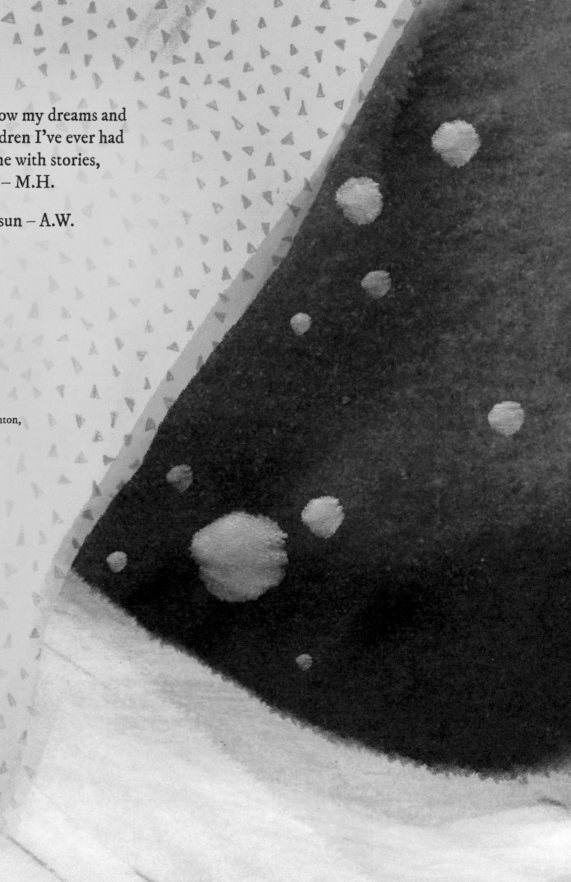

Until You Find the Sun

MARYAM HASSAN   ANNA WILSON

Crocodile Books, USA

An imprint of Interlink Publishing Group, Inc.

www.interlinkbooks.com

Aminah's life was
full of **sparkles** . . .

. . . from the golden sunshine to the juicy yellow mangoes Baba brought home, and the warm *salaams* of her friends.

Every night, Aminah's grandfather, Da, told stories of adventurers who went to new lands and made great discoveries.

And every night, Aminah listened,
her eyes wide, as she snuggled among
the cozy cushions on Da's *charpai*.

One day, Mama and Baba said,
"We're going on an adventure."

"Like in Da's stories?" Aminah asked.

"Come on, Da, let's pack our bags!"

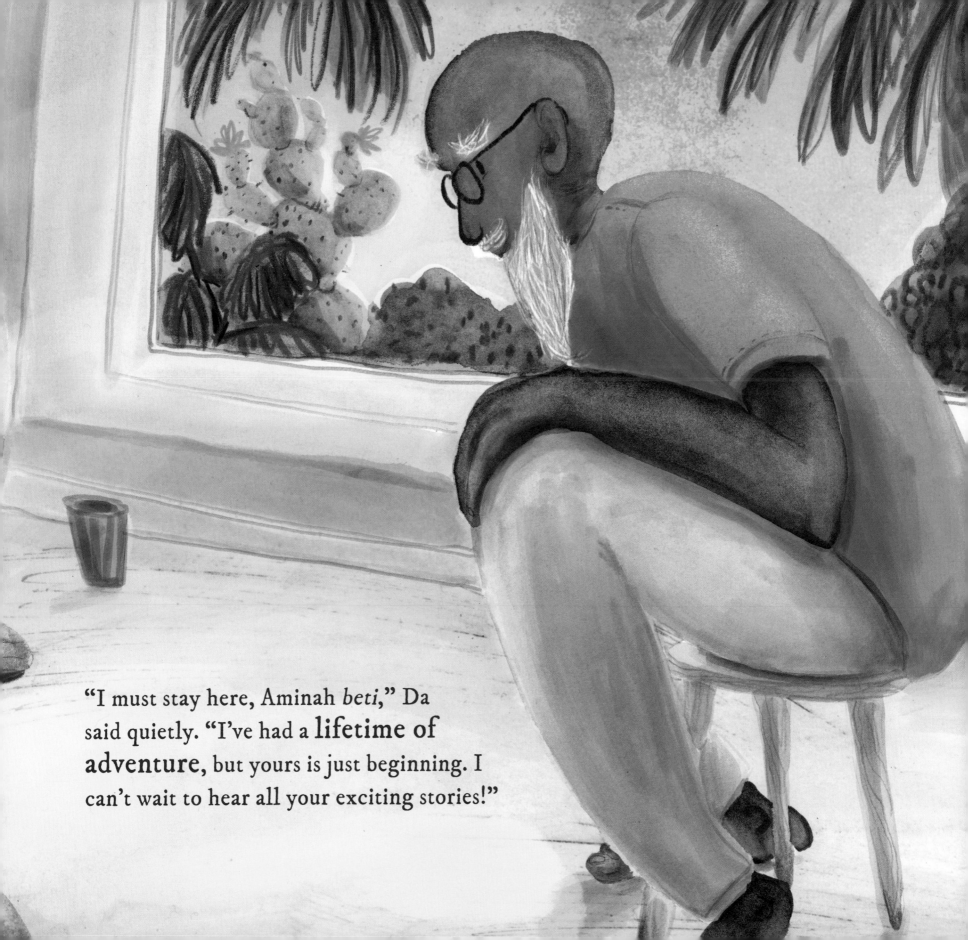

"I must stay here, Aminah *beti*," Da said quietly. "I've had a **lifetime of adventure**, but yours is just beginning. I can't wait to hear all your exciting stories!"

As weeks passed, the house became empty and still.
Da visited every evening until moving day.

When the time came to say goodbye,
Aminah held back tears.

"Aminah *beti*, you are **brave** like
your Baba. You are **fearless** like
your Mama. You are an **adventurer**
like me," Da reassured her.

"Can't you come too?" she
asked for the hundredth time.

Da hugged Aminah tight and said,
"I am always with you. You will
find sunshine wherever you go."

Aminah looked for bright
skies when the plane landed,
but she only saw gray.

There were no golden rays of sunshine,
no warm breezes to tickle her skin
and no smiling faces to greet her.

The car sloshed through damp
streets to their new home.

"This is no adventure,"
Aminah sighed.

For the next few days,
Aminah searched for the sun.
But the wind just blew cold
and bitter around her.

She had to wear so many layers
outside that she felt stiff as a robot.
The frosty air hurt her nose
and made her skin tingly and numb.

At Aminah's new school, everyone stared.
The teacher talked **too slowly**.
The children spoke **too fast**.

Mama and Baba tried to cheer Aminah up.
But her favorite food didn't
taste as yummy and her
best flowery dress didn't
make her feel brighter.

It was only Aminah's phone calls with
Da that could **fill her with warmth.**

Some days, it all felt too much.

"I AM COMING BACK!"
Aminah said to Da one night.
"It's too dark and too cold!"

"Your adventure is only just
beginning," said Da.
"Remember, I am always with you.
I will light your way **until you find
the sun again.**"

Aminah promised Da
she would try harder . . .

. . . but soon the weather turned colder, a cold Aminah had never felt before.

Outside, Aminah tried to hold Mama's hand tightly, but her mitten got in the way. Her coat was heavy, and her boots hurt her feet.

Just when she thought she couldn't walk any further, **something caught her eye** up ahead . . .

. . . a *yellow* from home.
Yellow like sunshine and mangoes
and the sweet-scented jasmine
that bloomed in Da's garden.

"Mama," Aminah whispered,
"please can I have it?"
Mama smiled. "Let's go inside."

Later, they called Da, and Aminah spun around in circles.

"You're brighter than the sun!" Da laughed.
"Now you light my way!"

The next morning, Aminah woke with a new glittering glow in her heart.

As she drew back the curtain, she was finally faced with the glistening sun she knew so well . . . but it was against a blanket of pure white.

"Da was right.
This is an adventure!"
Aminah whispered.

Aminah rushed outside and into the snow.

"I like your coat," said her neighbor.
"You are shiny like the sun!"

"It's always sunny where I'm from,
and blue skies stretch wide like an ocean,"
replied Aminah, proudly.

"You are the **yellowest sunshine** and
I am the **bluest sky!**" said the girl.
"Do you want to play with me?"

Together, they rolled
HUGE snowballs and
made perfect snow angels.

Aminah's nose
tingled with the cold,
but she didn't mind.

Later, Baba and Mama helped Aminah make her very
first snowman. They worked until the day grew dark and the
snow began to fall again in soft flakes all around them.

"This is Da!"
Aminah said, and
they all laughed
and laughed.

The snow fell heavier, like stars falling from the sky,
but for the first time ever **this new home didn't feel so cold.**

That night, Aminah called Da and told him stories of adventurers who went to magical wintry lands and played in the snow . . .

. . . that night, Da listened, eyes wide and heart full, knowing his granddaughter had **found her sunshine** again.

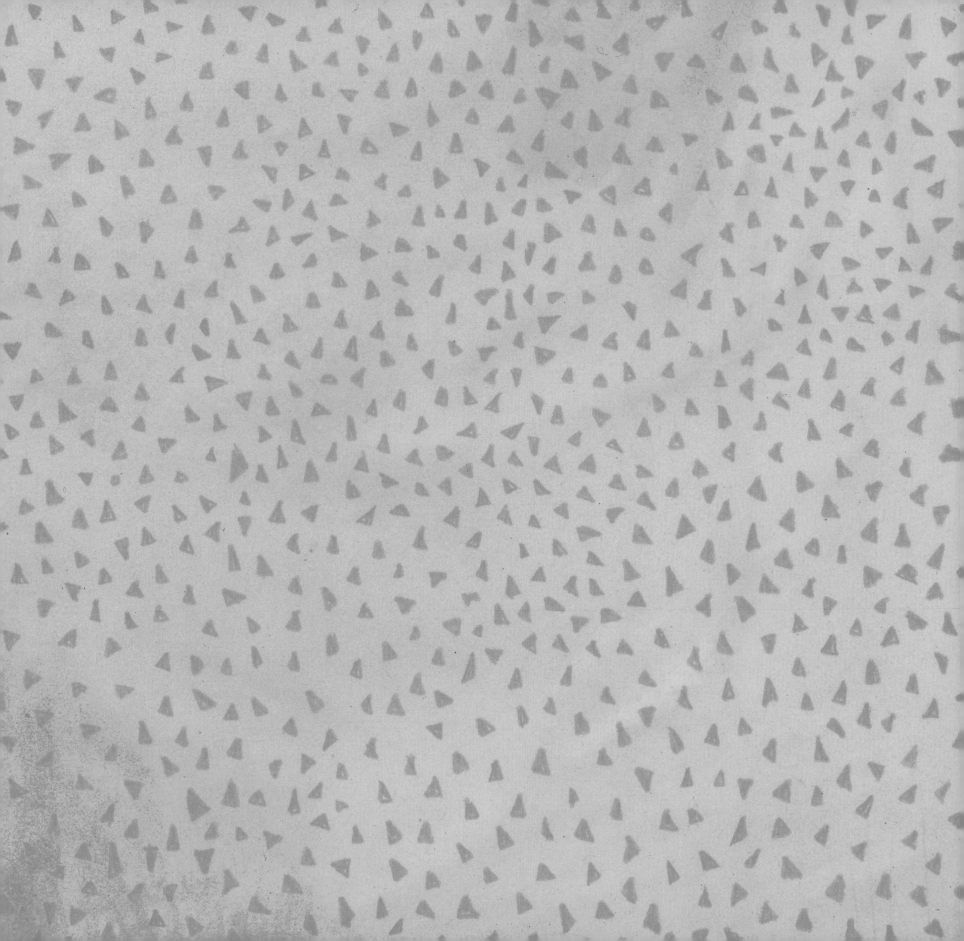